DONKEY DANIEL
in Bethlehem

LUKE 2:1-18 FOR CHILDREN

Written by
Janice Kramer

Illustrated by
Obata Design Inc.
Alice Hauser

ARCH Books

COPYRIGHT © 1970 BY CONCORDIA PUBLISHING HOUSE,
ST. LOUIS, MISSOURI

MANUFACTURED IN THE UNITED STATES OF AMERICA
ALL RIGHTS RESERVED
ISBN 0-570-06053-2

Nearby the town of Nazareth,
a long, long time ago,
there lived a little donkey
with a nose as white as snow.

His name was Donkey Daniel.
He was very strong indeed;
why, he could carry anything
that anyone might need.

He loved his master Joseph,
    who was gentle as could be.

He loved his cozy, little stall. He loved his favorite tree

But
Donkey Daniel
had a wish,
a wish he somehow knew
had very, very little chance
of ever coming true.

He wanted so to see the world,
to learn what lay beyond
the fences of his master's yard,
the neighbor's muddy pond.

"Perhaps behind those
distant hills," he thought,
"the sky is brown.
Perhaps the grass is pink.
Perhaps the trees grow upside down."

One morning master Joseph came
to Donkey Daniel's stall.
"I've brought your breakfast," Joseph said.
"Be sure to eat it all.

"Today we leave for Bethlehem,
   and you must come along
      to bring some things and carry Mary
         on your back so strong."

He stood impatiently as Joseph
started in to pack
the things he'd have to carry
on his sturdy little back.

First came a leather saddle,

then some bags of food and drink,

and a tiny sack of money—
he could hear the coins go "clink!"

Then Joseph lifted Mary up.
She seemed so very small
    that Donkey Daniel hardly felt
        her on his back at all.

"It's time for us to go," said Joseph.
"I will walk ahead."
And Donkey Daniel followed
where his gentle master led.

They passed the houses and the wall,
right out of town they went.
And when they reached the distant hills,
they started their ascent.

Straight up they climbed,
till Donkey Daniel
thought they'd hit the sky.
"Why, I can see
for miles around!"
he cried.
"Oh, my!
OH, MY!"

Then down they went, through valleys green,
    past laughing little streams.
"The real world," Donkey Daniel thought,
    "is better than my dreams."

They walked and walked for days,
and then, at last, one afternoon,
good Joseph cried, "There's Bethlehem!
We ought to be there soon!"

"That is good news!" said Mary.
Oh, how gladly she replied,
for she was very tired
from the long and bumpy ride.

The town of Bethlehem was filled
with visitors that day,
so Joseph had to look and look
to find a place to stay.

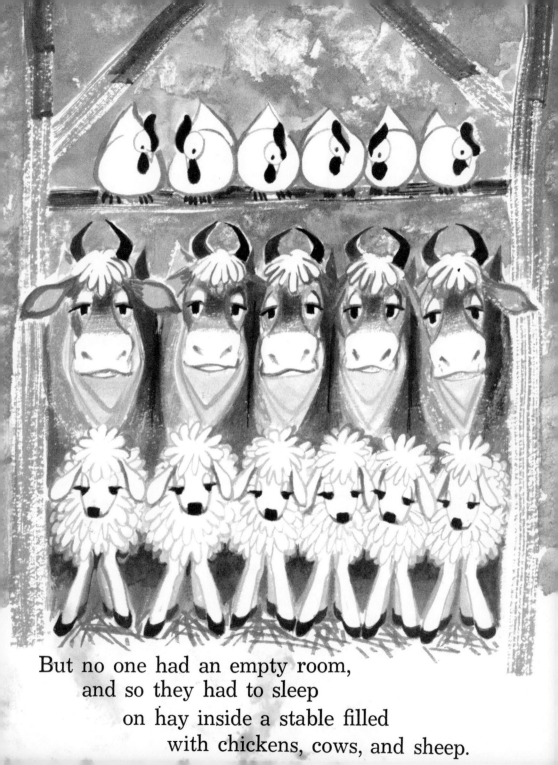

But no one had an empty room,
and so they had to sleep
on hay inside a stable filled
with chickens, cows, and sheep.

They ate their supper,
    made their beds,
        and shut the stable door.
Then Mary fell asleep, and Joseph
        started in to snore.

"Good night," said Donkey Daniel
to the chickens, cows, and sheep.
Soon all was calm and silent.
Everyone was fast asleep.

But Donkey Daniel wakened
in the middle of the night.
"How strange!" he mumbled.
"Mary's up. The stable's filled with light.

And Joseph, why is he awake?
Whatever can it be?
I must find out what's going on.
I must get up and see!"

He didn't quite expect to see
the sight that met his eyes.
"A BABY!" Donkey Daniel cried,
with wonder and surprise.

"Why, Mary's had a baby boy,
        and such a lovely child!
See there!
      He looked at me just then.
I think He even smiled!"

Then suddenly a knock was heard
            upon the stable door.
Three men came in, quite out of breath,
            and knelt upon the floor.

"We're shepherds,"
they explained.
"We've come to see the Son of God!"
"What do they mean?"
thought Donkey Daniel.
"This is very odd."

He tried to understand each word
       the happy shepherds said:
how angels had appeared to say
       that in a manger bed
they'd find the Son of God, a Child
       newborn of holy birth,
a Baby who was Christ the Lord,
       the Savior of the earth!

He tried but didn't understand
       the many words he heard.
How could a tiny, little babe
       be Christ, the mighty Lord?
But then a strange thing happened:
       something made him bow his head
before the Baby Jesus lying in the manger bed.

DEAR PARENTS:

The imaginary Donkey Daniel longs to see the great sights. His wish is to travel beyond his little world in the village of Nazareth.

His wish is finally fulfilled. He sees many new sights on the way to Bethlehem, but the greatest sight is a surprise. He sees the promised Saviour, Christ the Lord, a newborn Child.

Like the donkey, many children and adults want to see the world. The ancients wrote about the seven great wonders of the world. In these days of air and space travel many have their travel dreams fulfilled. It is a thrilling adventure to see many natural and manmade wonders in strange and distant places.

As our story shows, the greatest wonder of all is the coming of God in the form and flesh of a human Child. This is the "great and mighty wonder" we sing about in our Christmas hymns and carols.

Our story ends with Donkey Daniel bowing his head before the Child Jesus in the manger. This reflects the tradition in stories and carols that "ox and ass before Him bow," that even animals and nature recognised the mystery that in the Child of Mary God is made manifest in the flesh.

We hope our story will appeal to the imagination of your child. Use it to point to the true meaning of Christmas, that the Son of God came as a humble Child to share our lives, to take our sin and suffering on Himself, and to give Himself on the cross for our forgiveness.

THE EDITOR